Melinda

And The Class Photograph

Melinda
And The Class Photograph

by Deborah van der Beek

Carolrhoda Books, Inc./Minneapolis

Melinda
And The Class Photograph

"Next Friday, children, we'll have our class picture taken," said Ms. Wibbley, "so I want you all to look your best. Even you, Melinda. It would be nice to see you in a dress for a change."

"My name's Mel," said Melinda. "And I don't like dresses."

"You heard Ms. Wibbley," smirked Amy after school.
"You'll have to wear a dress, Melinda Gammon."

"Mel," answered Melinda. "And I'm not going to."

Harry was horrified. "Oh, but Ms. Wibbley said you have to."

"Huh!" snorted Melinda. "Nobody's going to make *me* wear
a dress."

Melinda's sister, Prudence, was getting ready for her ballet class. "I hear you have to wear a dress on Friday."
"I'm not going to," snapped Melinda.

"Look at what I bought Melinda," smiled Mrs. Gammon on Thursday evening.

"Ooh, isn't that pretty," cooed Prudence. "If it were two sizes bigger, I'd wear it myself."

"You can have it," growled Melinda.

On Friday morning, Melinda was searching for her sweatsuit.
"But it's filthy!" said Mom. "You want to look clean and pretty for the photograph, don't you?"
"No, I don't," said Melinda.

"But what about that lovely new dress?" protested Mom.
"Yuk!" said Melinda. "Anyway, it looks itchy."
"Nonsense," said Mom. "You put that dress on *immediately*, Melinda Gammon."
"Mel," muttered Melinda, and put it on.

On the way to school, it started raining. Melinda kept trying
to splash her new dress, but her mother pulled her away every
time.

"No messy games this morning," said Ms. Wibbley when the class was assembled. "We all want to look nice and clean for the photographer, don't we?"

Not if I can help it, Melinda thought. She crept into the storeroom and took down some paints . . .

"Who said you could do that?" demanded Amy. Melinda stumbled back and tripped over the steps.

"Help!" squealed Clare and Amy. But Melinda's dress was as white as ever.

It was circle time. Ms. Wibbley said, "Be careful with that juice, Melinda. It's very sticky, and it stains. And chocolate cookies are too messy for today."

Chocolate . . . messy? thought Melinda. Where's mine?

But Ms. Wibbley was too late. Harry had already handed the cookies around.

"Oh dear!" sighed Ms. Wibbley. "Chocolate cookies AND you've dropped the juice."

"Hello, everybody!" called the photographer. "Sorry I'm late."

"You don't look very clean and neat," Ms. Wibbley worried.
"Except for Melinda, that is."
Melinda sulked.

"Melinda Gammon, you said you weren't ever going to
wear . . ." began Amy.
"MEL," snarled Melinda.

"Come on," called Ms. Wibbley.
But Melinda wasn't listening.
She had spied her dog, Captain,
rolling in some mud. "Oh, I bet
that's smelly!"
Then Melinda remembered that she
had a dog biscuit in her pocket.

"Say 'sausages,'" called the photographer.
"Waaaah!"
"Oh, no, Captain," cried Ms. Wibbley.
"Ha ha!" laughed Melinda.
CLICK! went the camera.

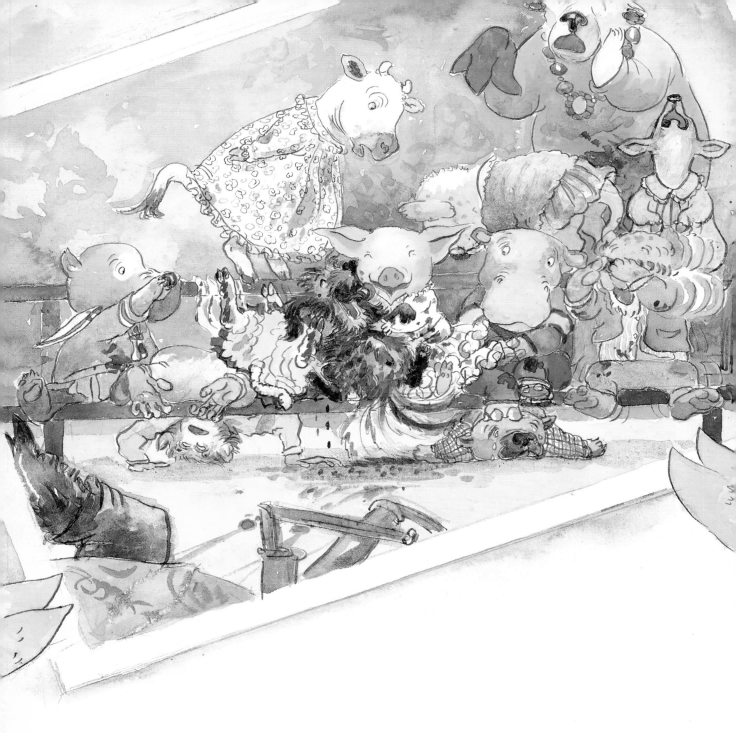

"In spite of the dirt, you look lovely, Melinda," admitted Mom when the photograph arrived. "What's a little dirt, after all . . ."

"Mel," said Melinda happily. "And do you know something? That dress wasn't itchy after all. In fact . . .

. . . Captain thinks it's very comfortable."

ABOUT THE AUTHOR

Deborah van der Beek was born and raised in London, England. From the time she was six years old, she knew that she wanted to be an artist. She studied ceramics at college and later worked as a gardener. Ms. van der Beek now lives in the tiny village of Lacock, England, with her husband and three young children, Henry, Theodora, and Bertie. In addition to *Melinda and the Class Photograph,* she has written and illustrated the *Superbabe* books.

This edition first published in 1992 by Carolrhoda Books, Inc.
First published in 1991 by Piccadilly Press Ltd, London.

Library of Congress Cataloging-in-Publication Data

Van der Beek, Deborah.
Melinda and the class photograph / by Deborah van der Beek.
p.   cm.
Summary: Unwilling to wear a dress for the class photograph,
Melinda tries her hardest to get it dirty.
ISBN 0-87614-694-9
[1. Behavior—Fiction. 2. Clothing and dress—Fiction.
3. Schools—Fiction.] I. Title.
PZ7.V2628Me 1991   91-20180
[E]—dc20   CIP
                                                                        AC

Manufactured in the United States of America

1 2 3 4 5 6 7 8 9 10 01 00 99 98 97 96 95 94 93 92